KU-661-393

ASH SURE WHAT OF IT

Publisher

Published in 2010 by Gregmar Books,
an imprint of Jetwood Limited

Limited Edition Copy

ISBN: 978-0-9566753-0-9

Author: Michael Cullen

Cover illustration and cartoons by Aidan Dowling

Design by Jamie Helly, Dynamo

Prepress by Impress Digital

Printed and bound in Ireland

ASH SURE WHAT OF IT

Michael Cullen
Cartoons by Aidan Dowling

Introduction

"There's terrific merit in having no sense of humour, no sense of irony, practically no sense of anything at all. If you're born with these so-called defects you have a good chance of getting to the top" – Peter Cook

To all those funny folk near and far who inspired us with their takes on life and beyond, many thanks. Although we have no wish to bow to political correctness, we have tried to observe some decorum and even a dollop of reasonable taste by avoiding overtly crude, sexist and racist jokes. For those anxious to be so amused, there's always the web.

While the inspiration for the content of this book has been largely Irish, it would be wrong not to salute the pioneers of the greatest one-liners, particularly those many American wits who excelled in put-downs. From Groucho Marx, WC Fields and Dorothy Parker to Joan Rivers, Woody Allen, Bill Hicks and David Letterman… the list is lengthy.

Closer to home, comics like Spike Milligan, Tommy Cooper and Dave Allen made us fall about for years, while nowadays the stage is there for Billy Connolly, Peter Kay Dara Ó Briain and Des Bishop to turn life on its head and make so many people feel the better for it.

British comedian Tim Vine is proof that the quickfire gag has returned. Vine won a prize at the Edinburgh festival for the funniest one-liner: "I've just been on a once-in-a-lifetime holiday. Never again." His other jokes include "One armed butlers, they can take it but they can't dish it out" and "Tequila! Schnapps! Sambuca! I'm calling the shots."

As for the comedy snobs out there who can't stomach puns, remember that a good pun is its own *reword*. It was the acclaimed American entertainer Oscar Levant who once said that "a pun is the lowest form of humour – when you don't think of it first."

Or as the Boston-born comedian Fred Allen (*née* John Florence Sullivan), most famous for his comical feuds with Jack Benny on air for years, remarked in 1948: "Hanging is too good for a man who makes puns, he should be drawn and quoted."

So for anyone who thinks puns are no fun, let's hope you never find yourself driving on an icy, abandoned road in the dark of night only to notice a road sign with half of it torn clean off – because that would be a bad sign. Rather, may the mirth be with you.

– Michael Cullen

HOLDING A NOTE
LONGER THAN ANGLO

When Brian Cowen became Taoiseach, Ireland was on the edge of an economic precipice. ***Since then the country has taken a giant step forward.***

What weapon destroys people but leaves banks standing?
The Financial Regulator.

A **BP** cocktail?
Three billion gallons of crude on the rocks.

Ashes to ashes,
dust to dust
what is Ireland
if not bust?

How can Europe be facing years of air chaos from ash if we're all struck on the ground?

Cheryl Cole was told at the British Airways check-in that she couldn't fly because of ash...
She asked what the little shit had done now.

It's a little early for volcano jokes.
We should really wait for the dust to settle.

Sign outside the National Concert Hall:
'Any tenor can hold a note longer than Anglo'.

How does Neven Maguire prepare his chickens?
He just tells them straight out they're going to die.

Money isn't everything, as long as you've got your health you can always sell a kidney.

The next meeting of Athlone clairvoyants is cancelled due to unforeseen circumstances.

Hedgehogs – why can't they just share the hedge?

Fianna Fáil has a great chance of winning the next election but only if they change the rules and turn it into a raffle.

THE F.F. ELECTION RAFFLE

Two BMWs crash. A dwarf gets out of one car and shouts at the other driver: *"I'm not happy."* The other driver replies: ***"Well then, which one are you?"***

MARTY MORRISSEY HAS A FACE WHICH CONVINCES YOU THAT GOD IS A CARTOONIST.

Jesus saves,
he's the only one who can afford to these days.

Todd Palin has been saving frantically for a sex change. *No matter what Sarah says, she's going to have it.*

The Bermuda Triangle got tired of warm weather and moved to Lapland. *Now Santa Claus is missing.*

Irish banks will lend money to anyone who can prove they don't need it.

Eamon Dunphy gets enough exercise these days, just pushing his luck.

NUDITY POSES NO PROBLEM FOR RIHANNA AS LONG AS SHE KEEPS HER RADIO ON.

A stand-up comic? Someone with a good memory who hopes none of their audience has the same sense of recall.

Remember Tesco shoppers, every Lidl helps.

While on a tour of Sweden, Jedward found a big lump of Plasticine in their dressing room, but they didn't know what to make of it.

The expletatron?
Tommy Tiernan swears by it.

HOW DO YOU MAKE HOLY WATER? BOIL THE HELL OUT OF IT.

Eileen was a trapize artist –
but she was let go.

David Norris knows what looks good on a woman but he will never want to take it off.

What happens if a lawyer takes Viagra? He gets taller.

Animal testing is horrendously cruel. The little mites get all nervous and give the wrong answers.

If Barbie is so popular, *why do you have to buy her friends?*

The government should nationalise crime, ***that way it won't pay.***

St Peter's Square – everyone knows that.

JEDWARD: WHAT TO MAKE OF IT...

SIGN IN EYRE SQUARE:
'Two hours on a Galway hooker, only €20'.

They discovered oil off Dalkey Island.
It drifted there from the Gulf of Mexico.

Ryan Tubridy

enjoys using self-deprecation, even though he says he's not very good at it.

MICHAEL NOONAN LOOKS LIKE A KINDER EGG WITH NO TOY INSIDE.

A Fifa referee will never be asked to launch the Round Ireland yacht race. He wouldn't be able to say which boats crossed the line.

TWITTER MESSAGE: 'ALEX HIGGINS DEPARTED FOR HEAVEN AROUND MIDDAY ON JULY 31ST 2010. **Months later, still no sign. Getting anxious, Peter.'**

Yvonne Keating has a talent for bird impersonations, *she watches Ronan like a hawk.*

Fox hunting would be a great sport, if only the fox had a gun.

Denzel Washington keeps his TV in his fridge. *How cool is that.*

THE WORLD'S FASTEST GAME?
PAST-THE-PARCEL IN A TEL AVIV RESTAURANT.

Thinking outside the box? Russell Brand doesn't even realise there is a box.

Making a speech is like visiting a nudist camp.
The first few minutes are hardest.

Emile Heskey was played out of position in South Africa – *by about 6,000 miles.*

A marketing expert?
Someone from out-of-town with slides.

IT'S EASY TO DISTRACT MARY HARNEY. IT'S A PIECE OF CAKE.

An Irish exorcism? *Having to call the devil to get the priest out of your son.*

Australia's prime minister doesn't speak French. ***Such is life.***

IF THOMAS EDISON HADN'T INVENTED ELECTRICITY, WE'D HAVE TO WATCH CORRIE BY CANDLELIGHT.

Voluntary work?
Most folk wouldn't do it if you paid them.

Whitney Houston's singing sounds like a bluebottle caught in the curtains.

THE GREENS SAY THAT BECAUSE OF GLOBAL WARMING THE WORLD'S OCEANS WILL RISE BY FOUR AND A HALF FEET. THIS CAN MEAN ONLY ONE THING, VAN MORRISON IS GOING TO DROWN.

The ESRI tells us business is looking up. That's because it's flat on its back.

If Vincent Browne wants your opinion, he'll give it to you.

The FAI? **Find Another Irishman.**

Avoid laughing on radio – you'll only sound like John Bruton being tickled with a cattle prod.

A psychiatrist? *Someone who goes to the Folies-Bergère and studies the audience?*

A guy went into the Petstop Superstore to buy a goldfish. The shop assistant asked him if he wanted an aquarium. He replied: "I don't care what star sign it is."

A skeleton walked into a bar in Kinsale and ordered a pint of Murphy's and a mop.

IF YOU LOOK LIKE YOUR PASSPORT PHOTO, YOU'RE TOO ILL TO TRAVEL.

Peter File avoids getting paged in the Shelbourne.

Sarah Ferguson,
now there's a lady with a sting in her tale.

SMALL AD: **'Laois man, 55, wants to meet woman with tractor. Send photo of tractor.'**

Abu Hamza is not great at interviews.
His hook makes everything seem like a question.

Herpes can be cured if treated early, so can kippers.

APPLE IPHONE, IPAD, IPOD, MACBOOK PRO and MAC DESKTOP. There's your five a day.

The last mosquito that bit Shane MacGowan *had to book into the Rutland Centre.*

SLEEPING WITH PROSTITUTES IS LIKE MAKING YOUR CAT DANCE WITH YOU ON ITS HIND LEGS. YOU KNOW IT'S WRONG, BUT YOU TRY TO CONVINCE YOURSELF THAT THEY'RE ENJOYING IT AS WELL.

Why's Nigella Lawson so cool?
On winter nights she makes you bake.

SOUTH AFRICA HAD AN ARCHBISHOP WHOSE NAME IS A BALLERINA COSTUME.

Macho? Jogging home after a masectomy.

Therapy is expensive. Popping bubble-wrap is cheap. You choose.

Revenue has got what it takes to take what you've got.

If ignorance is bliss, why aren't there more happy people?

Abandon hope – Pandora took the money.

"IT IS FORBIDDEN TO THROW TANTRUMS ON THE LINE."

Sign in Athenry train station:
'It is forbidden to throw tantrums on the line'.

Barack Obama slept with his mum until he was ten. He must have been very tired.

Eddie met his missus in a singles bar, which came as a surprise to him as he thought she was at home minding the kids.

How do we know Jesus wasn't English?
He wore sandals without socks.

Sign outside St Vincent's Hospital:
'Family planning advice – use rear entrance'.

How is it that whenever someone mentions Ivor Callely, *Pinocchio comes to mind?*

Lily Allen phoned David Lloyd Leisure to see if they would teach her how to do the splits. ***They asked her how flexible she was and she said any day but Saturday.***

A snail was mugged by two slugs in Fairview Park. The Garda asked him to describe his attackers. He said: *"Well now, that's a tricky one, it all happened so fast."*

If rhino horn is an aphrodisiac, how come the rhino is an endangered specie?

SOME PEOPLE THINK THEY'RE SMART TAKING DRUGS – *LIKE CUSTOMS OFFICERS.*

A monkey in a minefield? **A baboom**.

The price of Prozac doubled last year. *Prozac users' reaction was "whatever..."*

LEONARD COHEN IS SO OLD THEY CANCELLED HIS BLOOD TYPE.

Tomorrow's weather will be Michael Jacksony. *It will start out dark and get lighter as the day goes on.*

How will we know when the recession is over? *When new car registrations for the year outnumber the seasons.*

WHEN NEW CAR REGISTRATIONS
OUTNUMBER THE SEASONS

An idea for 'Your Country, Your Call'?
Give money to street beggars who knock food out of fat people's hands.

South Africa has a new noisy trumpet.
It's called the Tutuzela.

THINK DAVID CARUSO. THINK DAVID MCWILLIAMS.

Kylie Minogue is like a teabag. You never know how strong she is until she's in hot water.

SAMUEL BECKETT WAS SIPPING A COFFEE OUTSIDE BEWLEYS. THE WAITER ASKED HIM:
"Are you waiting for gateaux?"

Bertie Ahern is a great listener.
He listened to the developers who told him not to listen to the economists.

George Hook wanted to join the school debating team but he was talked out of it.

Ardal O'Hanlon saw a sign by the road side that said 'Tiredness can kill'. He never knew that. Only recently, he stayed up watching films. He could have died.

If crisps lovers have fat fingers, why don't P&G make Pringles tubes bigger?

CIARÁN WENT TO THE SPECIAL OLYMPICS IN SEMPLE STADIUM BUT THERE WAS NO PARKING FOR MILES.

Political spin doctors complaining about the media is like sailors complaining about the sea: rough.

Where did Lech Walesa meet his wife?
At a Gdansk.

KERRY KATONA THINKS PLATO IS A GREEK WASHING-UP LIQUID.

A bigamist? *A blanket of fog in Rome.*

Telepath wanted. ***You know where to apply.***

THE LAST TIME WAYNE ROONEY MET THE QUEEN AT BUCKINGHAM PALACE HE TOLD HER KIPLING WAS "EXCEEDINGLY GOOD".

If Willie O'Dea can't laugh at himself, he could be missing the joke of the century.

What do you call a Gulf of Mexico dolphin? ***Anything but Slick.***

IF PORN RELIEVES SEXUAL TENSION WHY AREN'T COOKBOOKS GIVEN TO THE HUNGRY?

How do you recognize a former Provo? He doesn't have tattoos where he rested his Armalite.

Dana's new show goes out at 8pm Sundays. So does everyone else.

It's always darkest before dawn – *a good time to steal your neighbour's newspaper.*

A **BIG MAC** walks into a bar and asks: "*Do you serve food?*" The barman replies: **"No, get lost!"**

They say love is blind, but then why is Ann Summers so popular?

News 24, ***go to bed.***

ANYTHING FOR 3 POINTS

Mick McCarthy was caught speeding on his way to Molineux. He'll do anything for three points.

Daffy Duck walks into a chemist and asked for a tube of ChapStick. The cashier says: "*That'll be €1.50 please*". Daffy replies: ***"Put it on my bill."***

THERE'S ONE THING ABOUT SEAN MONCRIEFF'S BALDNESS, IT'S NEAT.

George Michael was a Boyzone fan until he discovered it was a band and not somewhere backstage.

Anti-ageing cream is God's little way of punishing the stupid.

Traffic lights were stolen in Roscommon. A Garda spokesman said some criminals will stop at nothing.

Greg Norman and Chris Evert were married by a judge. *They should have asked for a jury.*

BORIS JOHNSON'S idea of passion? Someone who can make it to the end without vomiting.

DO NOT WALK BEHIND ME, FOR I MAY NOT LEAD.
DO NOT WALK AHEAD OF ME, FOR I MAY NOT FOLLOW.
DO NOT WALK BESIDE ME, EITHER.
JUST LEAVE ME ALONE.

Why do women in burkas take photos of one another?

What will prisoners in Thornton Hall use to contact their mates? ***A cell phone.***

Heterosexuals who hate homosexuals should stop having them.

Fisher-Price is to market a Dáil chamber doll.
You wind it up and it nods off.

DÁIL CHAMBER DOLL

THE X
MARKS-THE-SPOT
FACTOR

Is Pat Kenny right wing, left wing or middle of the bird?

SILVIO BERLUSCONI IS AS SLIPPERY AS AN EEL DOUSED IN LUBRICANT.

Two cows in a field. One asks the other: "*Are you worried about mad cow's disease?*" **"No,"** the other cow replies, ***"I'm a badger."***

Lindsay Lohan was Snow White but then she drifted.

IF QUIZZES ARE QUIZZICAL, WHAT ARE TESTS?

Shirley Temple Bar
finds cooking for one a drag.

Perhaps the FF-Greens coalition should plead contemporary insanity.

Little girl, little girl where have you been?
I've been to London to model for Queen
Little girl, little girl what did you there?
Stood around, leapt around, jumped around, bare
Little girl, little girl, what happened then?
Nothing – they're funny these cameramen

Tony Cascarino MAY NOT BE ON TV3 MUCH LONGER. HE'S OFF TO NIGERIA TO COLLECT HIS LOTTERY WINNINGS.

BEING POLITICALLY CORRECT MEANS ALWAYS HAVING TO SAY YOU'RE SORRY.

The US has declared war on Iceland
for possessing weapons of ash disruption.

SIGN OUTSIDE THOMOND PARK: *'Fans who make anti-Islam chants will see their names on the sects' offenders list'.*

Angelina Jolie found childbirth terrifying. Doctors say the response is common among Western women who realise they are about to have their baby in Africa.

RAOUL MOAT WAS THE ONLY ENGLISHMAN TO GET THREE SHOTS ON TARGET DURING THE WORLD CUP.

Brian Kennedy would never rummage through a woman's drawers.

Edward Cullen condones every Type O behaviour.

"TYPE O" BEHAVIOUR

Written beside the gap on the line at Tara Street train station: '**BEWARE LIMBO DANCERS**'.

Liveline callers don't grow on trees. They usually swing from them.

The greatest invention was the second wheel. People look stupid on a monocycle.

Jam made from strawberries is strawberry jam.
Jam made from raspberries is raspberry jam.
Jam made from rhubard is rhubard jam.
Jam made from gooseberries is gooseberry jam.
Why then is jam made from oranges called marmalade?

THINK ADRIAN CHILES. THINK BENNY HILL.

Maggie Simpson
wants an unbreakable toy for Christmas because it's handy for breaking other toys.

Black Beauty – he's a dark horse.

We're told Dow Jones is up or down. Why don't they just leave the man be?

Dublin taxi driver to Tony O'Reilly while they were passing Harcourt Street Railway Station after it was shut down by CIE chairman Todd Andrews: ***"Sure he'd close down the stations of the cross."***

People don't swim in Galway, they just go through the motions.

Winona Ryder *was spotted in Superquinn balanced on the shoulders of a couple of vampires. She was charged with shoplifting on two counts.*

Need a cure for erectile dysfunction? *Click on Floppywilly.com.*

DANNY BOYLE will only join a club which allows him to dismember.

AS SOON AS LUCY GAVE UP EATING BANANAS HER DIET WENT PEAR-SHAPED.

WINNIE MANDELA. SHOULDN'T IT BE LOSIE MANDELA?

Rejoice, Larry King has retired. No more nights of watching an angry sea turtle.

Daragh had a job in a bowling alley. Tenpin? No permanent.

Kinky sex with chocolate? **S&M&M**.

TERRIFIC - NOW BOTH BRIDES ARE LATE.
GAY WEDDINGS

Eileen has an eight-year-old retriever named Stay. When he was a puppy, she would call him: "Come here, come here Stay."

SIGN OUTSIDE BORZA'S TAKEAWAY: 'Insult Ireland's chipperati and you get battered'.

Samantha Mumba
says the press write a lot of silly things about her – ***Mumba jumbo***.

If you think you're too small to make a difference you've never been to bed with a female mosquito.

The OJ Simpson website? SLASH, SLASH, BACKSLASH, ESCAPE.

What kills 99 per cent of all known computer germs? **MS Dos**.

DAVID JAMES should quit football and try his hand at tap dancing.

If the French won't buy our lamb, we won't use their letters.

History will be kind to Jeffrey Archer – he intends to write it.

IUD? LOVE SPRINGS ETERNAL.

MONAGHAN POTHOLES...

The potholes in Monaghan are so big that if motorists drive in a straight line the Garda think they're drunk.

If Teri Hatcher gets any thinner, the other housewives will use her to floss their teeth.

THINK EVELYN CUSACK. THINK JOAN BURTON.

Why do women wear tights? Look what they do to bank robbers' faces.

There are so many Chinese walls in Irish business there are rickshaws lined up outside.

KEEP DU
GIVE MICK WA

UIN TIDY.
LLACE A HAIRCUT

Throughout his teenage years, Alan Carr had to wear a brace. In fact, his teeth were so big that if he had gone to Africa on safari he would have been poached.

Psychiatrist to patient:
"So you think you're a potato. On the couch please".

Mary Coughlan does the work of two men – Ant & Dec.

Bride's dad handed the groom a note:
'Goods delivered are not returnable'.

Groom handed a note to bride's father:
'Contract void if seal is broken'.

GOODS DELIVERED
ARE NOT RETURNABLE

A fire broke out in Arsenal's Emirates Stadium. Arsène Wenger shouted: *"The cups, save the cups!"* The fireman said there was no need for alarm, the flames hadn't reached the canteen yet.

Question for Birdwatch Ireland
– *have hummingbirds forgotten the words?*

Derek Mooney
is hard to ignore but it's well worth the effort.

Three out of every ten Irish men have a problem with premature ejaculation. *The others don't see it as a problem.*

A racehorse is the only animal that can take thousands of people for a ride at the same time.

Pilot asked permission to land his plane and said: *"Guess who?"* Controller switched the field lights off and replied: ***"Guess where?"***

A SIPTU BOSS IS TELLING HIS YOUNG SON A BEDTIME STORY: "ONCE UPON A TIME-AND-A-HALF…"

The trouble with *Ulysees*? The covers are too far apart.

Invaders From Mars is banned on the Garvaghy Road. No Martian, end of story.

George W Bush went into Burger King and asked for two whoppers. The man behind the counter said: *"You're an intellectual giant and the best US president ever."*

Saoirse Ronan, be wary of any film director with Roman in his name.

FATHER JACK ARRIVED AT THE WEDDING DRESSED AS THE CADBURY'S GORILLA. ***THE BRIDE AND GROOM TOLD GUESTS IT WAS A BLESSING IN DISGUISE.***

Ballygowan was the top bottled water in Ireland before Perrier had lead in it.

Man walks into Body Shop and shouts out: "I've already got one!"

Could Caster Semenya be a male Bride of Frankenstein?

Paul Gascoigne shook hands with Daniel O'Donnell and his whole right side sobered up.

HOW DO YOU KNOW YOUR GOLF GAME IS IMPROVING? YOU HIT FEWER ONLOOKERS.

Forget about Head & Shoulders. Procter & Gamble should market flavoured dandruff.

Homer Simpson – nobody d'ohs it better.

A LONG WAY TO TIPPERARY?

IT'S A LONG WAY TO TIPPERARY? EVER TRY FLYING RYANAIR TO PARIS, OR BARCELONA, OR…?

What does Brendan Grace see when he looks in the mirror? ***A row of toilet cubicles partly obscured by a fat man.***

A guy walks into Belfast Zoo. Every cage is empty apart from one which has a dog in it. *"What's going on?"* he asks the zookeeper. *"Read the sign,"* the zookeeper replies, ***"it's a shitzu."***

Aoife makes clown shoes – which is no small feat.

Sheriff Woody Pride has been hanged and is in a state of suspended animation.

The Bible says any man who sleeps with another man should be stoned. *Most men would agree it definitely helps.*

Eloquence? A man's ability to describe Miriam O'Callaghan without using his hands.

A Cockney walking down a street in North London sees three Spurs season tickets nailed to a tree. "Ey, I'll have them," he says to himself, "you can never have enough nails."

TWEET FROM MOTEL 666: ***"Kagame, Kim Jong Il, Karadzic, Mugabe and Netanjahu, left light on 4u"*** – Hitler, Stalin, Mao, Pinochet, Amin, Pol Pot, Ceaucescu and Saddam.

Kenny Rogers has had more tucks than a Jury's Inn bedsheet.

Sign outside shoe shop in Darwin: *'Beware of Crocs'.*

Never take a blind date to a silent movie.

Rob Green went into the England dressing room with his head in his hands – and dropped it.

Bear Grylls's cousin? Wolf Stir Fry.

BAVARIA, YOU'VE BEEN TANGO'D.

PIZZA FASTER THAN THE GARDA

WE LIVE IN AN AGE WHEN PIZZA GETS TO YOUR HOME FASTER THAN THE GARDA.

Why on earth do the winners of Miss Universe always have to be from this planet?

Ronnie Whelan

hates graffiti. He hates all Italian food.

Hey Bosch, how come there is a light in the fridge and not in the freezer?

Nicolas Sarkozy wanted to be a judge but they discovered his mum and dad were married.

Two lions doing a weekend shop in SuperValu? One turns to the other and says: ***"Quiet in here today, isn't it?"***

WE LIVE IN AN IRELAND WHERE LEMONADE IS MADE FROM ARTIFICIAL FLAVOURS AND FURNITURE POLISH COMES FROM REAL LEMONS.

Ads for Persil show how it removes blood. But if you have a shirt full of blood stains, maybe laundry isn't your problem.

HOW IS IT THAT THERE ARE SO FEW LAPSED PROTESTANTS?

Senator Donie Cassidy as Hamlet? "Toupée or not toupée..."

Kids who want a dog for Christmas should start out by asking for a horse.

PARIS HILTON YEARNS FOR A MEANINGFUL OVERNIGHT RELATIONSHIP.

Psychiatrist to patient: ***"You have emotional problems and a low IQ, I'm going to prescribe*** *EastEnders.*"

Halitosis is better than no breath at all.

BILLY CONNOLLY'S EPITAPH: 'JESUS, IS THAT THE TIME ALREADY?'

A Dundalk fan on the terrace in Oriel Park: *"Get stuck in, Dundalk!"* Another fan from the back: ***"We are stuck in Dundalk."***

BP should have a word with Jackie Healy-Rae about capping their oil wells.

Does Brendan O'Connor commit acts of random kindness?

GO, HARVEY GO. GO AND GET RID OF THOSE AWFUL ADS.

Why doesn't Mexico win more Olympic medals? All the Mexicans who can run, jump or swim are already in the US.

If you're being chased by a Garda dog, try not to go into a tunnel, then on to a little seesaw, then jump through a hoop of fire. Jimmy Carr says they're trained for that.

PAEDOPHILES – WHAT IS IT ABOUT BEARDS AND GLASSES THAT KIDS FIND SO ATTRACTIVE?

Strategy should be good enough to show off, just like a good bra.

What's black and white and hungry?
Heath Ledger's cat.

... IT'S ONLY NOW HE CAN
TALK ABOUT IT.

SEÁN QUIT AS A MIME ARTIST.
It's only now he can talk about it.

How did JFK feel about women's rights? It so happened he liked either side of them.

Darth Vader

knew what Luke Skywalker was getting for Christmas. He felt his presents.

NAOMI CAMPBELL HAS AN ABOVE AVERAGE QI.

Blind people should avoid skydiving
– it scares the hell out of their dogs.

Eamonn Holmes overweight?
Never. It's just that TV can sometimes give the wrong impression.

STAMP COLLECTORS MAY NOT KNOW MUCH ABOUT PHILATELY, BUT THEY KNOW WHAT THEY LICK.

Graham Norton blamed the volcanic ash on the cow who jumped over the moon.

IT'S NOW BEYOND DOUBT THAT CIGARETTES ARE THE BIGGEST CAUSE OF STATISTICS.

THE TORY PARTY IS THE CREAM OF BRITISH SOCIETY – THICK AND RICH AND FULL OF CLOTS.

Is acne an occupational hazard for footballers?
Like, Robbie Keane picks his spot.

Bob Dylan may soon have to rely on a Zimmerman frame.

Norwegian is German spoken underwater.

How much is shampoo in Dagenham?
Pantene.

How far away from the beach do togs become undies?
If you can't see the water you're in undies.

What profits a man if he gains the whole world and finds Mohammad cartoons funny?

Des Bishop promotes the ESB which is odd because he's a gas man.

Singapore is Disneyland with the death penalty.

ENDA KENNY IS EXTREMELY MODEST. HE HAS EVERY REASON TO BE.

PUTS ANY BABY TO SLEEP

I'M OFF
CHAMPIONS LEAGUE

Samantha Cameron's memoirs will be more boring than Anne Frank's. Excerpt: ***"Stayed in tonight, David cried."***

Ray D'Arcy is really popular in Cumbria and it's all due to radioactivity.

Vidal Sassoon went to the White House to do Michelle Obama's hair. The CIA agent asked him if he had a permit and he said no she only wanted a trim.

Make someone happy, bring Pat Rabbitte to the boil.

XMAS? It sounds like a skin complaint.

"THEY'RE GETTING THICKER BY DEGREES."

Elle Macpherson is one of God's finest achievements. So why isn't there one for every man in the audience?

If things don't work out for Thierry Henry at the New York Red Bulls, there's always basketball.

The wages of sin is death
and the wages at Dunnes are even worse.

GENTS TOILETS IN IRELAND ARE FRAUGHT WITH FIR.

Why did the jellybaby go to school?
BECAUSE HE WANTED TO BE A SMARTIE.

Joe trained in origami and opened a shop in Mullingar – **BUT THE BUSINESS FOLDED**.

RICKY GERVAIS is so ugly that when he goes into a bank the CCTV cameras switch off.

A Hindu mortgage? Paying off your home loan over several lifetimes.

What's worse than raining cats and dogs? Hailing taxis.

The peace process will be complete when the Wolfe Tones disband.

A baby seal went into the Gresham hotel. The barman asked him what he wanted to drink. The baby seal said: *"Anything but a Canadian Club."*

Britney Spears was never smacked as a child. Well, maybe one or two grams to get her to sleep at night.

If the Garda arrest a mime, must they inform him of his right to remain silent?

A PERSON'S SEXUALITY IS DETERMINED AT BIRTH AND CAN'T BE ALTERED WILLY-NILLY.

When an FAI spokesman opens his mouth, it's only to change whichever boot is in there.

Bart Simpson thinks Bach is something Santa's Little Helper does.

A MAN TRIED TO KIDNAP A JAPANESE TOURIST OUTSIDE TRINITY COLLEGE. THE GARDA HAVE HUNDREDS OF PHOTOS OF THE SUSPECT.

Amy Winehouse's surname sounds like a description of her liver.

NEW ZEALAND'S ARMY? LORD OF THE RINGS.

TALLY-HO? THE NUMBER OF SLAGS ON A HEN NIGHT IN TEMPLE BAR.

TALLY-HO!

RUSSELL CROWE HAS LAUNCHED HIS OWN WEBSITE TO REFUTE STORIES ABOUT HIM IN THE MEDIA. CHECK IT OUT AT LIKEWEREALLYCARE.COM.

Dáithí Ó Sé once felt like a man in a woman's body – ***then he was born***.

A lorry full of tortoises collided with a van full of terrapins just outside Kilkenny. It was a turtle disaster.

When has a dog dropping more impact than a bomb dropping? When the dog dropping is on your doorstep and the bomb drops in China.

Seamus died from the Big C.
It hit him after it fell off the front of Centra.

Our neighbour is such a bad cook his wheelie bin has developed an ulcer.

Curiosity killed the cat but for a while Lee Harvey Oswald was a suspect.

Cuban? It's a lot like Spanish but with fewer words for luxury goods.

IRISH ALZHEIMERS?
YOU FORGET EVERYTHING BUT THE GRUDGES.

A chick in a white shellsuit? An egg.

BRIAN KEENAN

Brian Keenan stops a Dublin taxi and sits in the passenger seat. The taximan turns to him and asks: ***"Sorry mister, but would you not be more comfortable in the boot?"***

Yoga? If God wanted us to bend over, he'd put McDonald's vouchers on the ground.

Voicemail message: 'For marijuana, press the hash key'.

IF THINGS GET ANY TOUGHER FOR THE WINDSORS LET THEM EAT CORGI.

Ondine: Not enough fish to fry
and not enough woman to love.

Why do they put photos of criminals up in post offices? Are we supposed to write to them? Why don't they put their mugs on stamps so the postmen can look for them on their deliveries?

Maeve Binchy has given more pleasure in bed than any woman.

BI-POLAR? Aaron Lennon thinks it's taking corners with either foot.

If all is not lost, where is it?

An Amish man with his hand up a horse's backside? *A mechanic.*

AN AMISH MECHANIC

Could the government not collect tax from people willing to watch Sean FitzPatrick and Michael Fingleton getting fired out of a cannon?

Tiger Woods favours affirmative action for women. ***A woman says action, he says affirmative.***

Iran has Shiria Law which isn't too kind to women. ***Britain has Jude Law***.

Oedipus, text your mum.

Portsmouth FC were no better equipped to survive in the Barclays Premier League than a Solero in the Sahara.

Anyone who believes in the Virgin Birth is labouring under a misconception.

Mr Whippy was found on the floor of his van covered in hundreds and thousands. ***The Garda said he topped himself.***

Does Beverley Flynn have delusions of adequacy?

Janelle Monáe's favourite treat? Galaxy.

Count Dracula, your Bloody Mary is ready.

"IT'S A HIL
FOCU

ARY CLINTON
GROUP."

THERE WAS A YOUNG MAN IN FLORENCE
TO WHOM ALL ART WAS ABHORRENCE
SO HE GOT SLIGHTLY TIPSY
WENT TO THE UFFIZI
AND PEED ON THE PAINTINGS IN TORRENTS

If John O'Donoghue was two-faced, why would he wear that one?

STATS ARE A LITTLE LIKE A BIKINI. WHAT THEY REVEAL IS SUGGESTIVE BUT WHAT THEY CONCEAL IS VITAL.

Whenever Stephen Hawking feels blue, *he starts breathing again.*

Alan's family had quick sand in the back garden. He was an only child – eventually.

Fabio Capello and Postman Pat may look similar but Pat always delivers.

If lawyers are disbarred and clergymen defrocked, does that mean electricians are delighted, musicians denoted, models deposed, dry cleaners depressed and cowboys deranged?

Spike Milligan was a psychic amnesiac. He knew in advance what he'd forget.

Avoid bumping into Roy Keane in Aldi. He has a stare that could melt a trolley.

What did the inflatable teacher say to the inflatable boy who took a needle into the inflatable school? You've let me down, you've let the school down, you've let your classmates down but worst of all you've let yourself down.

Simon chased a girl for two years only to discover that her tastes were similar to his – ***they both liked girls.***

No Pope in the Shankill. Lucky old Pope.

THINK JIM-JIM NUGENT. THINK DYLAN THOMAS.

Lisa's grannie didn't get to say goodbye before she died which was rather odd. *She drowned in a bowl of Cheerios.*

Is there no beginning to Eddie Murphy's talents?

THERE'S A NEW BREED OF DOG – A PIT BULL CROSSED WITH A ST BERNARD. IT BITES YOUR ARM OFF AND THEN GOES FOR HELP.

Lord Mandelson is about as straight as the Yellow Brick Road.

Very funny Scotty, now beam me down my clothes.

"VERY FUNNY SCOTTY..."

Never run over a Meath fan when they're on a bike – IT'S PROBABLY YOUR BIKE.

The Irish Bankers' Federation
– there's a typo there somewhere.

How do you get a camel through the eye of a needle? You start by running its hump through a meat grinder.

Dermot Ahern
could play Hangman for Ireland – he knows how to let people down.

LENNY HENRY CALLED PREMIER INNS' ROOM SERVICE AND ASKED THEM TO SEND UP A LARGER ROOM.

Being a Catholic doesn't stop you from sinning. *It just stops you enjoying it.*

The US? Where most people believe professional wrestling is real but 9/11 was faked.

Health nuts are going to feel stupid one day, lying in hospital dying of nothing.

Do Parisians play Scrabble with French letters?

IF YOU SEE A BANDWAGON, IT'S TOO LATE.

OIL SPILL
FOR M

.R. "GUSHING
NTHS"

Siobhán wishes she could drink like a lady
She can take one or two at the most.
Three puts her under the table
And four under her Come Dine With Me host.

When Kerry's Paul Galvin gets mad, you don't need a ref, you need a priest.

John knew he didn't get the job at Twitter when they didn't reply to his telegram.

What has 300 legs and seven teeth? The front row at a Cliff Richard concert.

They don't have American Express in Johannesburg, they have Joburg Express. ***The slogan is 'Don't Leave Home'.***

JEREMY CLARKSON HAS BEEN TOLD BY THE BBC TO KERB HIS EMOTIONS.

PHILOSOPHY IS LIKE A G-STRING. ***When taken to excess it disappears up its own posterior.***

Wether: a bad spell of weather.

Apathy ru…

An entrepreneur? Someone who walks down 12 back alleys and gets badly beaten up each time, only to repeat it again and again.

What have Stephen Ireland and a bottle of Miller in common?
They're both empty from the neck up.

A crèche? An accident in the Jack Lynch tunnel.

NEVER SHOW YOUR GUMS WHEN POSING FOR A PHOTO. IT CONJURES UP IMAGES OF WOLVES AND OTHER PREDATORS.

Why does the Foyle run through Derry? If it walked it would be mugged.

The only way Vanessa Feltz could crack the US is by sitting on it.

Nothing beats the great smell of Chanel – SO WHY NOT USE NOTHING?

Vindaloo purges the parts other curries cannot reach.

Ireland's country 'n' western capital? Youghal.

SIGN IN WEXFORD: Is an opera buff someone who reaches high notes naked?

Is the iPhone a must for techies? Appsolutely.

Jim McDaid denies being anti-semantic. Some of his best friends are words.

HOW MANY CREATIVES DOES IT TAKE TO CHANGE A LIGHTBULB? 100 – ONE TO CHANGE THE LIGHTBULB AND 99 TO SAY: *"I CAN DO THAT."*

Chef Keith Floyd was cremated. The service lasted for 30 minutes at gas mark six.

PROFANITY IS THE CROUTON OF AN INARTICULATE MUTHAFOOKAH.

Lynn Barber says Robert Redford's face looks like a child's sandpit after heavy rain.

Lady Gaga thinks monogamy leaves a lot to be desired.

Who helps Brooklyn Beckham with his homework?

WHY IS IT THAT THE ONLY PEOPLE WHO KNOW HOW TO RUN OUR COUNTRY ARE DRIVING TAXIS OR CUTTING HAIR?

THE ONLY PEOPLE WHO KNOW HOW TO RUN OUR COUNTRY...

The difference between a good and a great lawyer? A *good lawyer knows the law and a great lawyer knows the judge.*

If Revenue can bring one tiny smile to just one little face somewhere, someone has slipped up.

John Terry texted Wayne Bridge: *"Now that's how you play away."*

Sign in Delta economy class: 'In the event of the cabin decompressing, oxygen masks will drop from the ceiling and untangling them will annoy you before you die'.

VOLVO, VIDEO, VELCRO
– I CAME, I SAW, I STUCK AROUND.

Jesus loves black and white – but he prefers Jameson.

Germaine Greer no longer smokes in bed. Someone hid her pipe.

The inventor of crosswords? Clue: His first name is P something, T something, R.

Four Mexicans drowning? Quatro sinko.

Research on male attitudes to oral sex found that 70 per cent of men find it sexually stimulating, 20 per cent find it relaxing and one in ten enjoy the peace and quiet.

Angry waiter pursues diner for not tipping him with the cry: *"Sir, you forgot to tip me!"* The customer replied: ***"Don't chew glass, that's the only tip you're getting."***

What would Brendan Gleeson do if he lost his voice? Pray that silent movies make a return.

The worst thing about being homeless is that you can never enjoy camping.

Why aren't dogs good dancers? Because they have two left feet.

Ian Paisley was christened with a flame thrower. It was a baptism of fire.

John McCririck? A cross between Jabba the Hutt and Great Uncle Bulgaria.

In Hong Kong, Clive James went over his credit card limit like a pole vaulter.

GOMBEEN? A PROTEIN FOOD FOR THE BRAIN.

"THIS EARL
IS A E

-BIRD MENU
IG HIT."

GLOBAL COOLING FOR AL GORE

2010? THE YEAR THAT AL AND TIPPER GORE EXPERIENCED GLOBAL COOLING.

An oscillator? Someone from the Gaeltacht who eats donkeys.

Parachute for sale. Used only once, never opened, small stain.

Emo Philips has a useful stage tip. Avoid the edge.

What's brown and sticky? A stick.

TWO AGENCY EXECS DROPPED INTO THE UNICORN FOR LUNCH. THE MANAGER ASKED THEM IF THEY HAD RESERVATIONS, TO WHICH ONE REPLIED: ***"YES, BUT WE'LL TAKE A TABLE ANYWAY."***

The AAAA? A support group for drunks who drive.

Maria Sharapova makes more noise than a seal thrown into a jet engine.

Waterbeds cut down on adultery. Ever tried crawling under one?

It's best to avoid having a heart attack while playing charades.

Met Éireann issued a weather warning. *The weather was told not to do it again or there'll be trouble.*

Little John dreams of being an astronaut and landing on the planet ***Cameron Diaz***.

TUTANKHAMUN *has changed his mind and wants to be buried at sea.*

ISN'T IT ODD THAT THE NUMBER 11 ISN'T ONETY-ONE?

April 14th in Iceland? Plume's Day.

Airports use terminal to describe a passenger building – *is it any wonder people are scared stiff of flying?*

Precious knew she was an unwanted child when she saw that her bath toys were a toaster and a radio.

If women ran the world, there would be no wars, just intense negotiations every 28 days.

The National Lottery –
A tax on people bad at maths.

Leo Varadkar could go far as a travel writer. Why wait?

IRISH MEN DO CRY
– when assembling furniture from Ikea.

Organ donation is well and good but don't overdo it or you'll be run off your feet.

Graffiti outside UL: **WHO TOOK THE FIZZ OUT OF PHYSICS?**

ITALIANS' VERSION OF CHRISTMAS?
ONE MARY, ONE JESUS AND 33 WISE MEN.

Louis Walsh
has a phonographic memory.

As **Ray Houghton** might say, the days of good English has went.

Barbra Streisand is attractive – in a Mr Burns from *The Simpsons* sort of way.

If it wasn't for gay men, fat women would never get to dance at weddings.

MELON IS A GOOD FRUIT. You eat, you drink, you wash your face.

TOP DISCO HIT IN LIMERICK: GLOCK AROUND THE CLOCK.

Lassie goes into a hardware store and says: ***"I'd like a job please"***. The store owner says: *"We don't hire dogs, go join the circus."* Lassie replies: ***"What would the circus want with a plumber?"***

Getting a lecture from a property developer on business ethics is like having a leper give you a facial.

Michael McDowell is to comedy what Susan Boyle is to beauty pageants.

A royal family is an expensive way to be cruel to a small group of people.

Keith Richards has been stoned more times than an unfaithful Iranian wife.

THINK WILLEM DAFOE. THINK JOHN BISHOP.

Fed up with dull grey hair?
Get used to it, you're a squirrel.

Hw do u kp a txtr in suspense? Tell ul8r.

KIDS REALLY BRIGHTEN UP A HOME. THEY LEAVE ALL THE LIGHTS ON.

KIDS REALLY
BRIGHTEN UP A HOME

Micheál Martin was talking at UCD. He said times are kind of tough. He also said that Dermod Desmond is kind of rich, water is kind of wet and Joe Dolan is kind of dead.

Four ladies of a certain age were having lunch in a restaurant. The waiter came over and asked them: *"Is anything alright?"*

Inscription for Muhammad Ali's grave:
"You can stop counting now, cause I've no intention of getting up."

Peugeot has a new bike called the Cantona. It gets off on a two-footed kick start.

JOE RESIGNED HIS JOB AT THE HELIUM GAS FACTORY. HE REFUSED TO BE SPOKEN TO IN THAT TONE.

The FedEx workout? When you absolutely, positively need to be slim overnight.

ONE SHOULD TRY EVERYTHING AT LEAST ONCE, EXCEPT INCEST AND LINE DANCING.

Susan Sarandon couldn't make the Oscars. She was at the birth of her next husband.

An MBA? A master of bugger all.

In Heaven, the police are Irish, the cooks French, the lovers Italian and it's all organised by the Germans. **In Hell, the police are French, the cooks Irish and the lovers German and it's all organised by the Italians.**

Sinéad O'Connor does as much for the image of convent education as Angela Merkel does for hang-gliding.

Two snowmen in a field near Birr. One looked at the other and said: *"Can you smell carrots?"*

You look at Whoopi Goldberg and you think to yourself, was anyone else hurt in the accident?

SPECIAL OFFER ON 'I LOVE YOU ONLY' VALENTINE CARDS. BUY TWO AND GET ONE FREE.

If Charlie Bird wanted a friend in Washington he should have got himself a dog.

Hugh Grant can out-act any telephone kiosk you care to mention.

Paul Scholes is to tackling what Herod was to babysitting.

NEWSHOUND
NOT JUST

IDN'T REALISE
UCH NEWSHOUND
AS IN REX

ARE FOR LIFE,
OR XMAS.

OH LORD ABOVE, SEND DOWN A DOVE
WITH WINGS AS SHARP AS RAZORS
TO CUT THE THROATS OF THOSE WHO TRY
TO LOWER PUBLIC SERVANTS' WAGES

Walkers should sign up *Avram Grant* for Monster Munch ads.

Life? Some days you're the pigeon and other days you're the statue.

Today, the biggest threat posed by Russia is getting trampled on by an oligarch's mistress in Harvey Nicks.

If women dressed for men, Penneys wouldn't sell much, just the odd sun visor.

If we're here to help others, what role does that leave the others?

John Waters thanks God he was raised Catholic, so sex will always be dirty.

Chris was a trampoline salesman – off and on.

Nudists wear one-button suits.

...THEN THEY VANISH.

BILL MURRAY BELIEVES IN GHOSTS AND MOST OF THEM ARE WAITERS. THEY TAKE YOUR ORDER, THEN VANISH.

A kangaroo walked into a bar in Kinnegad and asked the barman had he seen his brother. The barman said: ***"Well now, I don't know, what does he look like?"***

Tired and emotional Nasa astronaut: *"HOUSTON, IT'S JUST ONE SMALL DRINK FOR MAN, BUT I MADE IT A DOUBLE FOR MANKIND."*

Mark Lawrenson is depriving a village somewhere of an idiot.

Jim Corr got fed up with his aunts saying to him at weddings that he'd be next. Now he tells them the same at funerals.

Batman hit the Joker over the head with a vase and he went: *"T'pau!"*.
The Joker said: *"Don't you mean 'Kapow'?"*.
Batman replied: ***"No, I've got china in my hands."***

WHY DID DR HAROLD SHIPMAN CROSS THE ROAD? TO HELP A PATIENT FIND THE OTHER SIDE.

Remember, Michael O'Leary, a closed mouth gathers no feet.

The world's dullest job? A lyricist for Hare Krishna.

Steven Gerrard tried to join Combat 18 but his boot size was smaller than his IQ.

SOME PUSHERS SELL DRUGS ON HIRE PURCHASE – BUT ONLY TO THOSE WITH JOINT ACCOUNTS.

The Vatican is a house of pill refute.

The three stages of marriage – LUST, RUST and DUST.

What did morons do before South Park?

Robert De Niro named his son Raphael after the hotel in Rome where he was conceived. ***The boy must be grateful it wasn't the InterContinental.***

Keith Barry almost had a psychic girlfriend but she left him before they met.

Why do builders have see-through lunch boxes? To let them know if they're going or coming home.

CATS HAVE NINE LIVES WHICH JIMMY CARR SAYS MAKES THEM IDEAL FOR EXPERIMENTATION.

In LA, people are so vain mirrors have lovebites.

Jose Mourinho was an atheist until he realised he was God.

Brian doesn't believe in astrology.
He's a Sagittarian and they're sceptical.

GRAFFITI IN BRADFORD:
'The BNP is a National Affront'.

"Turn right... Wrong! I didn't say Sat Nav says..."

DON'T TELL ME WE'RE DOING AN AD WITH A BIKINI-CLAD GIRL DRAPED ACROSS IT?
SPEEDO

BUT IT'S AN AD
FOR BIKINIS...

What's the difference between a fairytale and a trucker's story? A fairytale begins 'Once upon a time…' and a trucker's story begins 'Now, this aint no shit…'

Zinedine Zidane's epitath?
It's better to have loafed and lost than to never have loafed at all.

Durex is the world's worst chewing gum – but what bubbles.

Hello Dolly, you're never alone as a clone.

**GOD MADE THINGS THAT CREEP AND CRAWL
BUT IRISH RAIL, IT BEATS THEM ALL.**

…BEATS THEM ALL.

Hallmark has launched a new greeting card in Austria that says congratulations for escaping from your underground sex hell.

Vladimir Putin is so oily that if he went for a swim in the Canaries, BP would have got off the hook.

British chancellor George Osborne is known as Boy George around Westminster. Everyone really wants to hurt him and make him cry.

A coach load of small photographers outside the Guinness Storehouse? The japarazzi.

Wogga-Wogga is an odd placename, but so too is Stepaside.

If Rice Krispies could talk they'd sound like Padraig Harrington.

Someone who cuts through a corner petrol station to avoid a red light? **An Esso-Asso**.

Kermit says time's fun when you're having flies.

ARMAGEDDON CHEESE – BEST BEFORE END.

The last wish of the Icelandic people?
To have their country's ashes spread over Europe.

When asked by Sky Sports for a quick word,
Alex Ferguson replied "velocity".

May the last clamper be strangled with the guts of the last traffic warden.

They say a man's personality is reflected in the car he drives. Does Craig Doyle have a car?

If Jimmy cracks corn and no one cares, how come there's a song about him?

DON'T WORRY ABOUT THE WORLD ENDING TODAY. IT'S ALREADY TOMORROW IN AUSTRALIA.

Why do more men die before their wives?
It's their choice.

Miley Cyrus is as pure as the driven slush.

Disney World? A people-trap run by a mouse.

Lyric FM over-fortifies the over-40s.

WHICH SIDE TO SPIT ON?

AN POST DROPPED ITS PROPOSED SERIES OF STAMPS DEPICTING FAMOUS IRISH LAWYERS AFTER THEY FOUND PEOPLE WERE CONFUSED AS TO WHICH SIDE THEY SHOULD SPIT ON.

A QUESTION FOR WHO WANTS TO BE A MILLIONAIRE: Who was the first person to look at a cow and say: ***"I think I'll squeeze these dangly bits and drink whatever comes out"***?

Why do croutons come in airtight packages? They're just stale bread.

Surely Shergar doesn't think horseshoes are lucky.

Tommy Cooper bought HP sauce. It cost him 6p a month over two years.

"It's okay Mom - I'm just re-li

ing the summer pop festivals."

There'd be less litter in Ireland if blind people were given pointed sticks.

Why's there no window in an aeroplane toilet? Who's gonna look in?

Ronaldinho is the only man alive who can eat an apple through a tennis racket.

Niall tried some of that aphrodisiac rhino horn. Now he gets urges to charge at Land Rovers.

Tony Blair has plans to write a mystery novel – or does he?

Tim Vine was in the army once and the sergeant said to him: "What does surrender mean?" He replied: "I give up".

Guinness Light was not a head of its time.

Monica Lewinsky's new book? *Me & My Big Mouth.*

Childbirth is like watching edited scenes from *Platoon*.

Sun readers – now there's an oxymoron.

Johnny Vegas says *"don't knock bingo... it's the only chance some people have of owning a giant ceramic cheetah".*

When Ian Wright was asked what he thought of Hamlet, he said he only ever smoked Marlboro Lights.

Why are farmers only buried three feet deep?
So they can still get a handout.

Ziggy Marley likes donuts – but wi' jammin'.

PLAYING IN THE PARK, LISA SIMPSON WONDERED WHY A FRISBEE APPEARED LARGER THE CLOSER IT GOT TO HER – THEN IT HIT HER.

I'M TAKING MY
USUAL THREE HOLIDAYS
THIS YEAR...

ME NEITHER.
ECONOMY: GLOOM

WHAT'S THE WILDEST THING A GROUP OF YOUNG ACCOUNTANTS CAN DO? GO INTO TOWN AND UNSUSPECTINGLY GANG-AUDIT SOMEONE.

SIGN OUTSIDE EGYPTIAN EMBASSY: **'There are Pharaohs at the bottom of our garden'.**

Terra firma is best and the more firma, the less terra.

Good girls keep diaries, Courtney Love doesn't have the time.

Think Mark Hughes. Think Barry Murph

What did Bing Crosby and Adolf Hitler have in common? Both were interested in other people's handicaps, both were obsessed with the masters race and both bade farewell in a bunker.

Dave Fanning entered a speed-reading competition but he hit a bookmark.

Why did the firefly burn to death?
It tried to mate with a lit cigar.

POLITICS IS THE WORLD'S SECOND OLDEST PROFESSION BUT IT'S NOT TOO UNLIKE THE FIRST.

Why did Robert Downey Jr snort NutraSweet? ***He thought it was Diet Coke***.

When in Rome, be an awkward bastard... and do what the Belgians do.

AMBIENCE? A NIGHT OUT WITHOUT POOR PEOPLE.

Jay Leno has more chins that the Shanghai phone book.

Irish drama rules, O'Casey?

Fans of Spencer Tunick, your end is in sight.

Furbling? Having to negotiate a maze of ropes at Shannon Airport even though you're the only person queuing.

Looking for a hairdresser in Edgeworthstown? *Check out Sherlock Combs.*

Richard Bruton looks more confused than a baby in a topless bar.

Does Charlie Sheen play around? Does Kelly Brook sleep on her back?

MALCOLM IN THE MIDDLE HAS TWO SCHOOLBAGS. HE'S BI-SATCHEL.

IS GORDON RAMSEY A FEW BEANS SHORT OF A CASSEROLE?

SIGN OUTSIDE BROWN THOMAS: 'Gucci, Gucci, Goo'.

What do you call a floating PC? *Dell Buoy.*

How come no one in beer ads has a beer belly?

THE CATHOLIC CHURCH HAS A TOUGH NEW POLICY ON CHILD MOLESTERS; THREE STRIKES AND YOU'RE A CARDINAL.

Michael Lowry's lips are sealed
– so are Ben Dunne's
and that's why he talks like that.

A HAUGHEY FLASHBACK?
A man with a Charvet shirt on back to front.

New sitcom on Al-Jazeera:
Men Behaving Baghdadly.

The Chinese are murdering pigs – go tell the RSPCA.

Carol's church accepts all denominations
– fivers, tenners, twenties.

Dara Ó Briain
says fighting terrorists is like trying to kill a wasp with a fridge.

LOVE YOUR ENEMIES JUST IN CASE YOUR FRIENDS TURN OUT TO BE A BUNCH OF BASTARDS.

The Dawn French diet? **Weight and see.**

Rugby hugger v Wag?
Hugger is more Louis XIV, Wag more Louis Vuitton.

Surprise the girl in your life.
Take her sister to Paris for the weekend.

Mafia wisdom: A friend is someone you call when you need to move house; a good friend is someone you call when you need to move a body.

HOW DOES A GERMAN EAT MUSCLES?
KNOCK, KNOCK, KNOCK. *AUFMACHEN*!

JONATHAN ROSS'S MOTTO?
Speech impediments wule UK.

There's a tribe in Papua New Guinea that worships the number zero. Is nothing sacred?

If your mechanic can't fix the brakes on your Toyota, get him to make your horn louder.

The angel said unto the shepherds,
"Shove off, this is cattle country."

CURED HAM. CURED OF WHAT?

Gentlemen prefer bonds.

Ireland's newest chain of Indian clothes shops
– *Whose Sari Now.*

How to kill off a Fossetts Circus show? Go for the juggler.

NOW THERE'S A BOY BAND IN GAZA.
NEW KIDS ON WHAT USED TO BE THE BLOCK.

Star Wars fans, metaphors be with you.

Margaret Thatcher will be buried not cremated.
The woman is not for burning.

A tuneful nerd? A Gleek.

Arthur gave up his seat for a lady – that's how he lost his job as a Dublin Bus driver.

Some clergymen weren't too upset when Michael Jackson died.
LESS COMPETITION.

Torvill and Dean are to become a comedy duo. Their first tour is Skitting on Thin Ice.

Moss Keane was once known as The Exorcist. He never went home until all the spirits were gone.

The Eskimo word for useless hunter? Famished.

When Gay Byrne was a boy, the Dead Sea was just sick.

GOD GAVE MAN A BRAIN AND A PENIS BUT ONLY ENOUGH BLOOD TO RUN ONE AT A TIME.

Listen out for the offshore forecast. It'll have you in knots.

Americans right to bear arms is slightly less crazy than the right to arm bears.

DYSLEXICS HAVE MORE FNU.

Packie Bonner got a girl into trouble.
He told her mum she watched *Ugly Betty*.

Steve Martin handed in a script and the studio didn't change one word. The word they didn't change was on page 85.

IF CORN OIL IS MADE FROM CORN AND VEGETABLE OIL IS MADE FROM VEGETABLES, WHAT'S BABY OIL MADE FROM?

Noel Dempsey visited a mind reader but he was given a refund.

Liam has ADD which is surprising because he drives a Ford Focus.

FUN-SIZED CRUNCHIES? You need at least six or seven of them before you have any fun.

If blind people wear shades, why don't deaf people wear earmuffs?

Patron saint of anorexics?
The Angel Gabriel for coming down to announce.

Telling a teenager the facts of life is like giving a fish a bath.

APPRENTICE BOYS OF DERRY – you're fired!

DUDE, I THIN
AN ONLINE
PROBLE
5/4
RAC
POS

. YOU'VE
AMBLING
.

I DON'T...

When asked how long it takes her to get her hair done, Dolly Parton replied: "I don't know, I'm never there".

Security was tight on the Ark. Noah insisted the woodpeckers were sedated.

What's orange and looks really good on al-Quaeda operatives? ***Fire***.

With Mick Jagger's lips, he could French-kiss a moose.

Keep Navan tidy – eat a pigeon a day.

THE GIRL WITH THE WANDERLY WAGON TATTOO.

RICH HALL SAYS A HOTEL MINIBAR ALLOWS YOU TO SEE INTO THE FUTURE: WHAT A CAN OF COKE WILL COST IN 2020.

Mary O'Rourke is writing a book. Well, she's got the page numbers sorted.

Mobile phones is the only topic where men love to boast about who's got the smallest.

Happiness is your dentist telling you it won't hurt and then seeing him catch his hand in the drill.

THE BEST SEX IS DURING A DIVORCE. IT'S LIKE CHEATING ON YOUR LAWYERS.

A cobra? Chest support for conjoined twins.

Why are the times of day with the slowest traffic called rush hours?

Four sheep tied to a post in Wales – a leisure centre.

Life's not fair. If it was, Elvis would be alive and all his impersonators would be dead.

Death is nature's way of telling us
to slow down or God's way of saying:
"HEY, YOU'RE NOT ALIVE ANY MORE".

Dennis Hopper's dying wish was to have his family around him. ***He might have been better off with more oxygen.***

Here's to absent friends – especially prosperity.

Change is inevitable,
except from a vending machine.

Is John Wayne dead? ***The hell he is.***

THE LAST SHALL BE FIRST AND THE FIRST SHALL BE LAST.
Good news for polar bears and penguins.

Last on the 50-things-to-do-before-you-die list? Shout for help.

The first three minutes of life can be dangerous.
The final three can be pretty dodgy too.

He who laughs last has not heard the bad news.

TIME FLIES BUT YOU'RE THE PILOT.

GOODNIGHT DAVID...
GOODNIGHT GOLIATH

Michael Cullen is editor of *Marketing.ie*, Ireland's marketing and media monthly magazine and is a regular contributor to Ireland's national media. As evidence that he has a sense of humour, he has been an Arsenal fan for over 40 years.

Raised by wolves, **Aidan Dowling** learned to survive by trading simple cartoon drawings for scraps of food. This he still does, contributing regularly to such magazines as *Phoenix*, *Marketing.ie* and *Private Eye*.